Highe and Higher

by
Alan Rogers

for Anna and Alice

PRINCETON ■ LONDON

Yellow Hippo bounces on her trampoline.

She can bounce as high as
her friends.

Yellow Hippo can bounce as
high as…

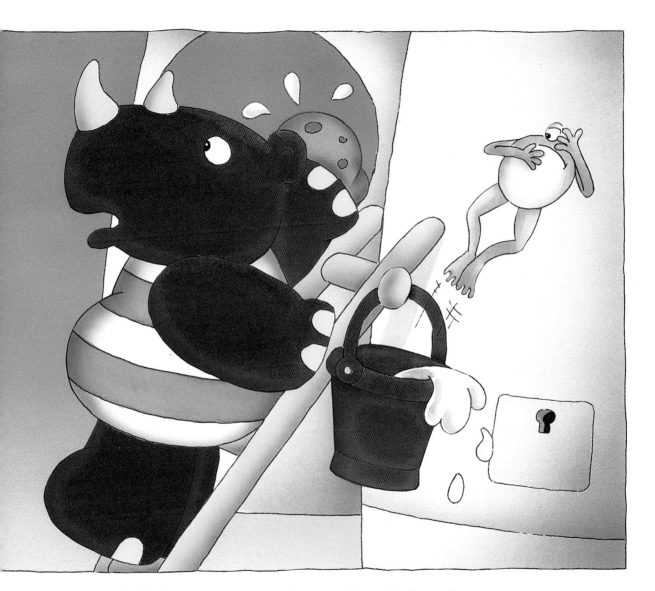

Red Rhino on his ladder!

Yellow Hippo can bounce as high as…

Blue Tortoise's window.

Yellow Hippo can bounce as
high as…

Green Bear can climb!

Yellow Hippo can bounce as high as…

the clouds!

She can bounce as high as...

a spaceship!

CLUNK!

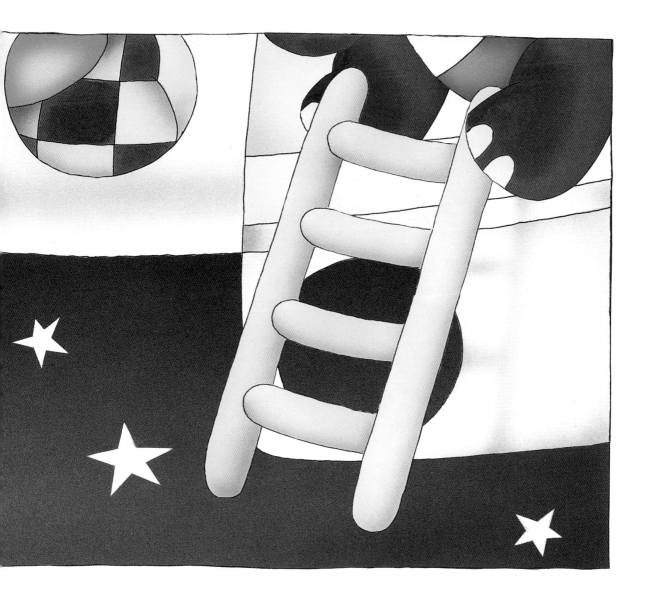

"Welcome aboard," say her
friends.

ZOOM!